CARRIED AWAY ON THE CREST OF A WAVE

also by David Yee

lady in the red dress
paper SERIES

CARRIED
AWAY
ON THE
CREST
OF A
WAVE

DAVID YEE

PLAYWRIGHTS CANADA PRESS
TORONTO

LIBRARY AND ARCHIVES CANADA CATALOGUING IN PUBLICATION
Yee, David, 1977-, author
 Carried away on the crest of a wave / David Yee.

A play.
Issued in print and electronic formats.
ISBN 978-1-77091-257-1 (pbk.).--ISBN 978-1-77091-258-8 (pdf).--
ISBN 978-1-77091-259-5 (epub)

I. Title.

PS8647.E44C37 2014   C812'.6   C2014-904101-2
C2014-904102-0

We acknowledge the financial support of the Canada Council for the Arts, the Ontario Arts Council (OAC), the Ontario Media Development Corporation, and the Government of Canada through the Canada Book Fund for our publishing activities.

For D & A, and all who suffered and all who lost.
And for those no longer among us.

FOREWORD

In our hyper-wired world of today, with its twenty-four hour news cycle, tragedies spread across our screens and around the globe at the speed of light. But how many random acts of cruelty can our spirits process, or even truly remember? In *carried away on the crest of a wave*, the wildly talented young playwright David Yee slows time to examine one such disaster intimately: the 2004 Indian Ocean earthquake and tsunami. The deadliest tsunami in recorded history, this disaster claimed roughly a quarter of a million lives, primarily in South and Southeast Asia. Yet, true to our times, even a catastrophe of this magnitude has receded from our memories, at least in North America, crowded out by a decade of more recent newsfeed items.

David Yee, however, refuses to let the many lives altered and destroyed drift into the recesses of our self-involved culture. An actor and playwright of Chinese and Scottish descent, born and raised in Toronto, Yee serves as the co-founding artistic director of fu-GEN, Canada's only professional Asian Canadian theatre company. He therefore stands at the forefront of a rich and blossoming genre, whose origins many trace to Canadian R.A. Shiomi's 1982 play *Yellow Fever*, which became a hit off-Broadway in New York and around the world. In 2010, Yee made a stunning playwriting debut with his full-length play *lady in the red dress*. Showcasing his exuberant theatricality and subversive intelligence, Yee mashed surrealism with mystery and genre elements to explore Canada's anti-Asian racist history, as well as the present-day denial of that past. *lady* was shortlisted for Canada's Governor General's Literary Award, marking the arrival of a major new theatrical voice.

carried away on the crest of a wave proves a brilliant follow-up to *lady*, demonstrating Yee's literary versatility, as well as his innate humanism and spirituality. A firm believer in the importance of research, he prepared by meticulously digesting everything he could find on topics such as earthquakes, fault lines, and the disaster itself. True of the best authors, however, Yee never shows his homework. In fact, the actual catastrophe itself is never depicted, but instead becomes the impetus for Yee to explore its impact on the lives and souls forever changed by its fury. These spirits are an eclectic bunch, spread around the globe: a Muslim engineer and a Catholic priest, two Japanese men falling down a seemingly endless hole, a radio shock jock in Toronto, a seismologist who blames himself for the Tsunami deaths, two brothers swept out to sea; a single natural disaster, rippling outward from its source, eventually reaching these disparate individuals, binding them into an unexpected community.

David Yee's *wave* therefore carries us to a wonderfully surprising place, where we glimpse the interconnectedness of all humanity. Perhaps his own vantage point, as a Western author of mixed-race Asian ancestry, gives him a unique perspective with which to appreciate a tragedy whose victims were overwhelmingly Asian. In any case, as a young author, Yee knows all too well how our screens and media hold sway over contemporary lives. Yet for that very reason, he continues to believe in the critical place of theatre and live performance in today's culture. In *carried away on the crest of a wave*, David Yee demonstrates the power of art to succeed where the facts and footage of our twenty-four hour news cycle often fail: to make palpable a human tragedy, mark its stories indelibly upon our memories, and bind us together as citizens of the world.

David Henry Hwang
Brooklyn, NY, 2014

PREFACE

This is a play about hope.

The 2004 Indian Ocean tsunami struck the coasts of fourteen countries spanning two continents over a period of twelve hours, beginning the morning of December 26th. It killed over 250,000 people from forty-six different countries, the deadliest tsunami in recorded history.

I have a friend who narrowly escaped while in Khao Lak, Thailand. In the days that followed, in the middle of the night, she would call me from the Thai hospital where she was convalescing. She'd recount to me what she was seeing, through a haze of painkillers, and those stories stuck with me long after she'd been discharged and returned home.

Over the course of five years, from 2007 to 2012, I read numerous accounts and conducted personal interviews with individuals and families who suffered tragic losses on that day, or who had miraculous stories of survival. . . sometimes both. An overwhelming number of them experienced moments of inexplicable coincidence, or profound intersection. Some of them even found hope. Not a single person I've spoken to has told me the story I'd expected to hear. The stories contained herein are not purely fiction, nor are they strictly fact. They are all, however, rooted in some common truth, shared experience or moment of unflinching honesty.

In 2011 I was at a conference in Xiamen, China, before heading to Thailand to do some first-hand research. While there, I wound up drinking with a Swedish girl I'd met at the conference. Mentioning sort of off-handedly where I was on my way to, she smiled knowingly and paused before saying, "I was there." She had been in Khao Lak as well. In fact, she'd been in the same hotel as my friend, only a few rooms apart. That's how small the world is.

From Patong Beach in Phuket you can see—very distinctly—the line along the coast where rebuilding has taken place. I wanted to take a picture, something detailed, but it was impossible to get the entirety of it in a single shot. If I walked farther back, I could see the whole landscape, but it was missing the detail, the sharpness I was looking for. Instead, I walked the perimeter of the line, taking several photographs that I could later edit together. It seemed a suitable metaphor for how I'd written the play.

It seemed impossible to sum up what happened on December 26, 2004, in a single narrative. Instead, *carried away on the crest of a wave* has an anthological structure: it's several short plays in a single container. This, to me, was the only way to approach it, the only way to capture the enormity of it while preserving a trenchant insight. That being said, every small play was written in reference to and in service of the larger structure. There are connections inside, between stories and characters, across the history and geography of the play. Some are obvious, but most require some excavation. The original Toronto cast referred to them as "Easter eggs" in rehearsal, things they would discover that connected them to others, expanding the world radially. None of the stories in this play stand alone, though they might seem to at first. Everything is connected.

Finally, this is not a definitive account of the 2004 Indian Ocean tsunami. There are so many stories that couldn't make it in; they were too unwieldy or took the play, as a whole, too off course. It also hasn't entirely finished *happening* yet. The tsunami set some events into motion which have yet to conclude. In December 2011, an Indonesian girl presumed dead found her way back to her village, seven years later, with only the vague memory of a café and one family member's first name to guide her. She was eight years old when she disappeared and it's still unclear how she survived or where she'd been for seven years. How many more, like her, are still out there?

This play contains nine stories. Stories about redemption, the impossibility of grief, loss, strange serendipity, brutality, sacrifice. . . but the play, as a whole, as the bottle these missives are preserved inside. . . this is a play about hope.

David Yee
Gold Coast, 2014

carried away on the crest of a wave was first produced by Tarragon Theatre in Toronto, Ontario, between April 24 and May 26, 2013. It featured the following cast and creative team:

Actors: Kawa Ada, Ash Knight, Eponine Lee, Richard Lee, John Ng, Mayko Nguyen and Richard Zeppieri.

Director: Nina Lee Aquino
Assistant director: Jenna Rodgers
Set and costume designer: Camellia Koo
Lighting designer: Michelle Ramsay
Sound designer: Michelle Bensimon
Stage manager: Joanna Barrotta
Assistant stage manager: Emilie Aubin

The play was first produced in the United States by the Hub Theatre in Fairfax, Virginia, between November 15 and December 8, 2013. It featured the following cast and crew:

Actors: Nora Achrati, Rafael Sebastian Medina, Ryan Sellers, Andrew Ferlo, Ed Christian and Hedy Hosford.

Director: Helen Pafumi
Scenic designer: Robbie Hayes
Lighting design:er Jimmy Lawlor
Sound designer and composer: Matthew Nielson
Costume designer: Madeline Bowden
Props designer: Suzanne Maloney
Stage manager: William Pommerening

CHARACTERS

Beckett
Swimmer
Runner
Amal
Ma'mar
Rick
Chili
Sanjay
The Hard-boiled Man
Kid
Crumb
Jasmine
Makoto
Kintaro
Nguyen
Lenore
Vermin
Diego

THE LEAP SECOND STORY

A press conference at the International Earth Rotation and Reference Systems Service, Australia. BECKETT, *a scientist in a lab coat, enters. She has a tablet computer that she refers to as she presents. The reporter she shared a moment with earlier in her day is in the audience.*

BECKETT: Ladies and gentlemen of the press.

Beat.

Especially gentlemen.

Beat.

Especially the gentleman in the blue coat who passed me in line earlier and brushed my shoulder and we both turned because a wave of electricity passed through us that was something like the feeling when you drink milk that's gone off, only good, and neither of us spoke but I wanted to tell you that you are the handsomest man I think I've ever seen.

Beat.

Thank you for joining us.

She clears her throat.

People often ask me what it is we do at the International Earth Rotation and Reference Systems Service. I think it's rather self-explanatory, but that's me. Over the years of being asked this question, I've simplified my explanation to the following statement: We observe.

This may blow your mind, but the earth changes speed and position constantly. Over the course of centuries the mean earth day has gotten longer, then shorter, then longer again. A number of factors are responsible for this. For instance:

On December 26, 2004, the earth's mass was drawn towards its core via tectonic subduction and the planet got. . . smaller. Because the planet got smaller, it started to spin faster, three microseconds faster than before. The day got shorter. But the force also tilted the planet 2.5 centimetres on its axis. It wobbled. Like knocking a spinning top, the tidal shifts created a "drag" effect, slowing us back down. The day got longer. These differences in microseconds may seem infinitesimal at the moment. . . but they *do* add up.

We, as scientists, as observers of anomalous planetary behaviour, as record-keepers of the "big picture," must account for these shifts and their impact on the future of our world. Like balancing a ledger, we—the accountants of time—have instituted necessary measures to maintain our pace with the earth. About every eighteen months, we add a leap second to Coordinated Universal Time. You aren't aware of it. But it's there. Inserted into the fabric of your day.

And by a marvel of science, a breakthrough in observatory technology that would take far longer to explain than we have tonight. . . for the first time ever, I can tell you what happened in that leap second. That fraction of a glimmer of the mere concept of a moment. You didn't even notice it. Because you weren't watching. But we were watching. And we wanted to let you all know. . . because if you know. . . then maybe we stand a chance after all. What happened in the leap second went something like this:

A balloon burst at a child's birthday party.
A mosquito pierced the surface of my skin.
Twelve people laughed at the same joke.
A plane lifted from the ground.
Two strangers shared a glance across a crowded subway car.
A match was struck to light a cigarette.
You smiled at me.
A phone rang once.
A honeybee disappeared into thin air.
Six people standing together all experienced déjà vu.

My face flushed at the sight of you.
A supercomputer finished calculating the end of pi.
A grasshopper swallowed a garden snake.
The Internet crashed.
Every child alive stopped crying.
California caught on fire.
There was peace on earth.
We fell in love.
The world ended.
And we were all reborn.

> BECKETT *puts the tablet down. She steps off the stage*
> *and into the audience. She finds the reporter in the blue*
> *jacket she shared a moment with earlier in her day. She*
> *stands him up, and kisses him.*

THE SWIMMING CHILD STORY

Malaysia. SWIMMER *and* RUNNER *are in a house. The house is in the ocean. Water quickly fills the house, rising from the foundation.* SWIMMER *and* RUNNER *are scooping it out with large basins and tossing the water out the window into the ocean.* SWIMMER *is bleeding from his head.*

SWIMMER: It's too much!

RUNNER: Your head!

SWIMMER: What?

RUNNER: Your head, it's bleeding.

SWIMMER: It's nothing.

RUNNER: It's a lot of blood.

SWIMMER: The head bleeds.

RUNNER: *Everything* bleeds.

SWIMMER: Not as much as the head.

RUNNER: How do you know?

SWIMMER: Do you remember last spring? Mother hit her head on the beam over there?

RUNNER: I don't remember.

SWIMMER: I remember. We drove her to the hospital.

RUNNER: Impossible. We don't have a car.

SWIMMER: We don't?

RUNNER: You probably saw that on television.

Beat. They realize together.

BOTH: The television!

They run to the television in the centre of the room, lift it together and heave it out the window. They assess the water situation. Still sinking.

RUNNER: Not enough.

SWIMMER: The sky!

RUNNER: What about it?

Short beat.

SWIMMER: I don't know.

RUNNER: Your head!

SWIMMER: It's fine, shut up! We should throw the television table.

RUNNER: We may need it.

SWIMMER: We don't have a television anymore.

RUNNER: We may need it as a *raft*.

SWIMMER: We may not need a raft if the house stops sinking.

RUNNER: Stop arguing with me!

SWIMMER: Stop making stupid suggestions.

RUNNER: Just find more things to throw.

SWIMMER grabs a trophy off the floor.

SWIMMER: Your running trophy.

RUNNER: Which one?

SWIMMER: *(looks)* The dash. One hundred metres.

RUNNER: Not that one. I like that one. Find the 10K, it's not as nice.

SWIMMER: This one is heavy. I'm tossing it.

He does.

RUNNER: No!

SWIMMER: You told me to find more things!

Beat. RUNNER picks up a trophy off the floor.

RUNNER: Fine. Then we should get rid of your swimming trophy. This one is from the match in KL.

SWIMMER: Not the nationals!

RUNNER tosses it out the window.

RUNNER: Good and heavy. Made a nice splash, did you see?

SWIMMER: Was that the television?

RUNNER: What?

SWIMMER: That made the splash?

RUNNER: Your swimming trophy.

SWIMMER: Oh no. . .

RUNNER: Your head. I think it's serious.

SWIMMER: Stop nagging me. You're as bad as Mother.

RUNNER: Stop being stubborn and I'll stop nagging.

SWIMMER: Find more to jettison or I'll throw *you* in.

> *They run around picking up more things and tossing them out the window.*

RUNNER: Photo albums.

SWIMMER: Books. Mother's books.

RUNNER: Those are my books.

SWIMMER: Wonderful stories, do you remember?

RUNNER: Not now, there's no time.

SWIMMER: One about the sky. . .

RUNNER: Keep going!

They keep picking things up and throwing them out.

CD collection.

SWIMMER: Collectable figurines and snow globes.

RUNNER: *Those* were mothers.

SWIMMER: Toys we used to play with.

RUNNER: More photo albums.

SWIMMER: Dog.

RUNNER: We don't have a dog.

SWIMMER: *Someone's* dog.

    Beat.

RUNNER: Is that it?

SWIMMER: Nothing more on my side. You?

RUNNER: Nothing.

    Beat. They return to scooping water out the window.

We should get out.

SWIMMER: We're safer in here.

RUNNER: We'll drown in here.

SWIMMER: Statistically we're safer at home.

RUNNER: Our home is sinking in the ocean.

> SWIMMER *falls to his knees; his face goes white and blank.*

Hey. Hey!

> *He kicks up some water at* SWIMMER's *face.* SWIMMER *wakes up.*

SWIMMER: What happened?

RUNNER: You passed out. Your head. . .

SWIMMER: Just tired, don't worry about me. It's been an exhausting day, what with the house being pulled into the ocean and all.

RUNNER: We can make the table into a raft. Take our chances; you need a doctor.

> SWIMMER *sits down in the water.*

SWIMMER: I just need a rest.

RUNNER: You never let me help you!

SWIMMER: Take a rest with me.

Beat. RUNNER *sits down next to him.*

It was a nice day, wasn't it?

RUNNER: It. . .

Beat.

You know what, it was. Not a cloud in the sky.

SWIMMER: Sky wasn't the problem.

Beat.

Sky. . . the sky. . . the sky. . .

RUNNER: Hang on.

SWIMMER: It's the sky. The. . . remember?

RUNNER: Your head. . .

SWIMMER: No. No no no. . . remember? It was in the book I just threw in the ocean. In the beginning. The very beginning. When the brothers were fighting over the throne of heaven. The god of fire. . . um. . .

RUNNER: Zhu Rong.

SWIMMER: And his brother. Gong Gong. The god of water. Zhu Rong won the throne, and Gong Gong was so angry that he went down to earth and smashed his head against Buzhou Mountain. . . the mountain that held the sky in place. He hit it so hard that it broke a bit and the sky started to fall. The world tilted and the great flood started.

RUNNER: It's a children's story.

SWIMMER: It's how the world began! The creator couldn't fix the mountain, so she had to cut the legs off the giant sea turtle Ao and use them to prop up the sky. Remember? The turtle holds the sky up, now. So something must have happened to it. . . to one of the legs. Something slipped maybe. And now the sky is falling down again.

Beat.

I can fix it. I'm a good swimmer. I'm the best swimmer. That's why I'm here, that's why the ocean grabbed our house and pulled us out. . . I have to help the creator fix the turtle's leg.

RUNNER: No. . . no, that's not what it means.

SWIMMER: It's okay. I'll ask Ao to balance the house on his back. You'll look down and see the back of the turtle who holds the entire world up.

15

RUNNER: I'll go with you. . .

SWIMMER: (smiles) That's not what you're for. I'm the Swimming Child and you're the Running Child. This is a job for the Swimming Child. You'll have your turn later. Don't worry.

He goes to the window and climbs halfway out of it.

I knew there was one more thing.

RUNNER: Please don't leave me.

SWIMMER: I'll be right back. I just have to go save the world. Won't take a moment.

RUNNER: I don't want to be alone.

SWIMMER: (smiles) You're not. None of us are. There's a giant sea turtle underneath us all. You'll see. We have to be strong. Can you be strong?

RUNNER nods. Beat.

Is my head really that bad, Runner?

Beat.

RUNNER: No. No, it's just a scratch. Like Mother when she hit her head on that beam over there. And we drove her to the hospital, with the dog in the back seat. It's just like that time.

SWIMMER: Yes. That's what I thought.

SWIMMER smiles at RUNNER, then dives out the window. There is a small splash. Beat. RUNNER sulks.

He measures the water. He scoops some more out the window. Measures again. Then again. The house has stopped sinking.

RUNNER: You did it. . .

He goes to the window. He looks down at the water. Then up at the sky. Then down at the water.

I can see your back. . .

He continues looking out the window as the sun begins to shine again.

THE SAINT STORY

*Basilica of Our Lady of Good Health in Velankanni,
Tamil Nadu, India. Father* AMAL *Thomas is blowing out
votive candles.* MA'MAR *Shaikh enters, timidly, carrying
small bags of electronic equipment. He stands off to one
side, admiring the interior of the basilica.* AMAL *watches
him for a moment, then approaches.*

AMAL: Peace, my son.

MA'MAR: Peace, brother.

AMAL: I have seen you circling around for days. I wondered if
you would land here.

MA'MAR: Ah. . .

AMAL: That was you, yes? The other day, with a metal detector
or some business, around the beach.

MA'MAR: Oh. Yes. . .

AMAL: Looking for buried treasure, were you? Find any?

MA'MAR: Oh, I wasn't. . .

AMAL: Don't keep it all for yourself, na. A small donation to the church is good for the soul.

MA'MAR: You misunderstand. . .

Beat.

I've been around, yes, taking density readings. . . I think you've been expecting me; I am the engineer—

AMAL: Yes! Yes of course! I'm so sorry, sir, you are so young. I was expecting an old man, you know the kind, thick glasses and. . . my apologies, you are here to *substantiate* our miracle!

MA'MAR: *(correcting)* Investigate.

AMAL: *(waves it off)* No matter. Welcome.

MA'MAR: *(extending his hand)* I am Ma'mar Shaikh.

> AMAL *is taken aback by the name. He looks at* MA'MAR's *hand, refusing to take it.*

AMAL: "Ma'mar *Shaikh*."

MA'MAR: *(a bit unsettled)* Um. . . I believe Monsignor Parish mentioned I would. . . he sent. . .

He retrieves a sheet of paper from his bag and hands it to AMAL.

AMAL: You. *You* are the expert.

MA'MAR: I am an architect and structural engineer. Top of my class at IIT and MIT in America. I designed the Citi Centre in Chennai, have you been?

AMAL: *(disdainfully)* Huh. Yes. The *shopping mall* everyone raves about.

MA'MAR: Thank you.

AMAL: Hm. I have been. The floors are uneven.

MA'MAR: They are?

AMAL: And the inside is too. . . fancy. So much *moulding*, na. Looks like a wedding cake.

MA'MAR: I'm sorry you feel that way.

AMAL: And the prices at Forever 21 are extravagant.

MA'MAR: I'm not sure that one is my fault.

AMAL: Che. *(waves the subject off)* You are the expert. . .

MA'MAR: I am told—

AMAL: You expect me to believe that the CCS, the *Vatican*, na. . . sent *you*.

MA'MAR: As I said, I was top of my—

AMAL: *(waves him quiet)* Yes, yes, you built a shopping mall, you are obviously a wunderkind.

Was there no Catholic available? Or even a Hindu (Lord, send me a Hindu!). . . but, *this*. . . a Muslim investigating a miracle for the Vatican. I do not believe this.

MA'MAR: I'm Ismaili. If that makes any difference.

Beat. It doesn't.

The Vatican has engaged the services of non-Catholics before, when necessary. There is precedence—

AMAL: *(scoffs)* "Precedence." First he's an architect, now he's a lawyer.

Beat.

MA'MAR: I am told that the event destroyed everything at this elevation, except your basilica. I am told that when the waves touched the statue outside, they stopped. I am told of two thousand people inside this room, not one pair of feet was wet. That, to me, Father Thomas, sounds like a miracle.

Beat.

But, I am also told. . . to investigate using science. Not faith.

AMAL: Science will prove faith.

MA'MAR: And yet, it is faithless. It is the same from a Muslim as it is a Buddhist or a Christian. Now, you don't want me here and I have a cricket match I could be watching, so why don't you show me to the site and we can both get on with our days?

Beat. AMAL *quietly acquiesces. He leads* MA'MAR *outside to the statue.*

AMAL: On Christmas Day, a young Japanese girl, a visitor to the basilica, placed a rosary on the hand of Our Lady. Not an uncommon practice, but this particular rosary had been blessed by Pope John Paul II. His holiness has not yet been canonized, but this miracle would ensure it. *(a commiserating aside)* It is. . . politic, you know? A story like this. . .

MA'MAR: Looks good on the brochure, yes?

AMAL: We have a saying: "It helps the flock to flourish."

They reach the statue. It is relatively unremarkable, but there are rosaries hanging off her hand.

MA'MAR: Was it this one, here? The rosary in question?

AMAL: No, no, this is a. . . placeholder. It was here that the water turned back, after touching the statue of Our Lady. The statue was undamaged, but the rosary was swept away. Our Blessed Mother reclaiming it, perhaps. There are many theories.

MA'MAR: *(considers this)* It is 325 feet to the shoreline, yes?

AMAL: Yes. The waves went miles inland, but the basilica and all in its shadow were untouched.

MA'MAR *feels the bottom of the statue. It's porous.*

MA'MAR: Sandstone for the base?

AMAL: You are the expert.

MA'MAR: I'd like to take some readings around here.

He begins to remove equipment from inside his bag, assembling a high-tech-looking device.

AMAL: I can only imagine what you think of this. . .

MA'MAR: Think of what?

AMAL: This statue. Our claims. Iconography of holy persons is forbidden by Islam, yes? So this statue, to you, this must appear to be incredible sacrilege.

MA'MAR: *(gives the statue a once-over)* Not one of our saints, so I suppose it's fine.

AMAL: Still, you must find the concept offensive or. . .

MA'MAR: I am Ismaili. I don't think anything of your statue, your crucifix or your medallions. I have a little St. Christopher in my car. He was there when I bought it. His head bobbles, it's very charming.

   Beat.

You know the Quran teaches us, "Revile not those unto whom they pray beside Allah lest they wrongfully revile Allah through ignorance."

   Beat.

Does your book offer a similar passage?

   Beat. AMAL *thinks.*

AMAL: *(changing the subject)* What are you building, there?

MA'MAR: It's like a sonograph machine for underground. It takes density readings of lower horizon levels.

AMAL *looks at him blankly.*

Okay, the ground under our feet is made up of layers—

AMAL: Che! I know!

MA'MAR: This machine tells me if the bedrock beneath us is more or less dense than the surrounding area. I graph it with the readings from along the coastline that you've seen me take, and it gives me a picture of what the upper ocean basin looks like.

AMAL: And what does all that have to do with our miracle?

MA'MAR: The graph will tell us. My machine is parsing this data with readings done from the Anna University Institute for Ocean Management and the National Institute of Oceanography in Goa. I'm connected already over WiMAX, so it will only take moments what would before take several days. Luckily. . . *(a little joke)* "there's an app for that."

He grins at AMAL, *who stares blankly back at him.*

AMAL: What?

MA'MAR: Um. . . an app for. . . like the iPhone.

AMAL: This is on your phone?

MA'MAR: No, it's. . .

AMAL: Are you calling them?

MA'MAR: It was just a little joke.

AMAL: Okay, very funny. App-something, okay. What about my miracle, na?

The machine beeps.

MA'MAR: The graph is complete.

MA'MAR looks at his screen.

Hm.

AMAL: "Hm"?

MA'MAR: I'm sorry, brother.

AMAL: Why "sorry"? What is there to be—

MA'MAR: This graph. . . it shows me there is a natural break-water leading from five miles out in the bay. . . running along either edge of the basilica. This. . . was no miracle. I'm sorry.

AMAL: You are making another joke, yes?

MA'MAR shakes his head.

My friend, there were two thousand eyewitnesses. *Dry* feet, na.

MA'MAR: Watch, watch. . .

MA'MAR gestures using the graph and his arms.

The waves start hundreds of miles out to sea. As they travel to land, their direction, their speed, even their shape is formed by the topography of the ocean basin. The breakwater acted as a barrier, directing the waves to either side of the basilica. All this sandstone soaked up the runoff. . . that's why no one's feet got wet. It is. . . incredibly *lucky*, what happened here. But miraculous? I'm afraid not.

Beat.

AMAL: My parishioners are. . . charitable. . . people. So blessed they felt when they were saved that they worked the next four days without rest, searching for survivors amid over eight hundred corpses. And do you know how far they got? One half a mile. A five-minute walk—eight hundred water-ravaged dead bodies. Many of them feel their lives have been *redefined* by this moment, this *miracle*. You can't just tell them it was luck. No, it was an act of God. A reward for their faith.

MA'MAR: Do you believe in God's plan?

AMAL: Of course—

MA'MAR: Then there you have it. It was in His plan for this to happen, for them to be saved—

AMAL: You don't understand—

MA'MAR: My brother, I do—

AMAL: As a Muslim, you have no concept of what the Catholic faith teaches us—

MA'MAR: Brother, please do not—

AMAL: I am not your brother!

MA'MAR: We are ALL brothers! And I am telling you, *my brother*, I know. And it is true, what I'm saying. The hand of God may not have come down to shield you from the waves on that day, but it was His will that formed a breakwater in the earth and His will when the basilica was built on it. You call him one thing, I call him another, but this is HIS work.

AMAL: So you are saying, this *was* a miracle. . .

MA'MAR: A miracle, no. But this, all of this, is the work of God.

AMAL: You mean "Allah."

MA'MAR: Does it matter?

AMAL: Of *course* it matters! Because *we* were saved, not Muslims, not Hindus, not Bahá'í, *us*.

MA'MAR: And you really believe what you should take away from that is that *your* God is the right God and everyone else is worshipping a false idol?

AMAL: Isn't that what *you* would do, if this had been a mosque?

MA'MAR: No, it isn't.

AMAL: Well then you're a bad Muslim.

MA'MAR: And you are an *excellent* priest.

Long pause. MA'MAR *begins packing up his equipment.*

AMAL: You don't have to do this. You could. . . you could just say you didn't find anything. You could say. . . and they'd believe you. I mean. . . that's something you could do.

MA'MAR: You don't really mean that.

AMAL: My people need hope.

MA'MAR: They have you.

AMAL: I'm not enough.

MA'MAR: They have their faith.

AMAL: And when that's not enough?

MA'MAR: It has to be. That's why they call it "faith."

AMAL: Brother.

Beat. MA'MAR *looks at* AMAL.

Please. . .

Beat.

MA'MAR: Do you know what it takes to be made a saint under Islam?

AMAL *looks blankly at* MA'MAR.

No. Of course you don't.

(deep breath) First of all, they're not called saints, they're called *wali*. . . this means "friend of Allah" or "walks with Allah." One test they use to determine if you can be a saint is that they dig up your body as many as six months after you die. And if the body is decomposing. . . you're not a saint. You are not faithful enough to walk with Allah.

I have family in Aceh. They are not poor, they live a good distance inland, so they weren't affected. But you saw eight hundred dead bodies that day? In Aceh there were over one hundred and fifty thousand. Most, if not all, of them were Muslim. I had been to *jamatkhana* with those people. They were *good* people, *pious* people. So many died saving others, men who'd made it to safety first, then gone back to rescue who they could. Died saving a person they didn't know. All they knew is this was someone's son. . . someone's husband. . . someone's brother. They put a stranger's life before their own. And not *one* of them was a saint? Those bodies all decomposed. . . they became bloated in water, skin sloughed off in sheets, their lifeless bodies were swollen and black and turning to sludge. . . because we are *men*. Just men.

And do you know what our leaders said? "Allah must have been angry. They must have been. . . bad Muslims." Do you see? Two hundred thousand dead. . . and it's used as a cautionary tale against us. Saying all of those people, all of them, were bad. . . because they decomposed. The way anyone would.

And now you want me to say that God worked a miracle on your Catholic basilica because someone put a string of beads on the statue of a woman? You want me to say those two thousand people standing on a breakwater were *better* than the two hundred thousand who died in Aceh? Is that what you're asking me to do?

Beat.

AMAL: I. . . I am asking you. . . to protect these people's faith.

MA'MAR: At what cost, Father?

Beat.

AMAL: *(shakes his head)* My father told me never to get into a theological discussion with a Muslim.

MA'MAR: Smart man.

AMAL: He said, "They are relentless, Amal. But we. . . we are *right*."

MA'MAR: *(smiles)* Maybe you are. Just. . . not today. I'm sorry, Father.

> MA'MAR *shoulders his bag and extends his hand to* AMAL, *who again doesn't take it. He is just staring at the statue of Our Lady.* MA'MAR *shakes his head and begins to walk away when* AMAL *finally speaks.*

AMAL: You know my name, my surname, "Thomas." This name comes from a saint. St. Thomas. One of the original apostles of Christ, and the first to preach Christianity in India. He has a church *(He waves his hand to indicate.)* in Chennai. Near to your shopping mall, maybe. Anyway, I've always liked St. Thomas. Maybe because of the namesake, I've just always felt. . . close. . . to him. Do you understand what I'm describing?

MA'MAR: A kinship.

AMAL: Yes. A kinship.

> *Beat.*

You know what St. Thomas is the patron saint of?

MA'MAR: I don't.

Beat.

AMAL: Architects. He's the patron saint of architects.

Beat.

Isn't that funny?

MA'MAR: Yes. I suppose it is.

> AMAL *looks at* MA'MAR, *a great weight in his eyes. He reaches out his hand.* MA'MAR *takes it.*

Peace, brother.

AMAL: Peace, my son.

> MA'MAR *exits.* AMAL *continues standing by the statue. He is racked with grief. He puts his hand on the statue to help him stand as he composes himself. After a moment, he notices his hand is wet. He looks at the statue of Our Lady. She is weeping. The statue is weeping.*

THE RADIO STORY

Toronto. December 28, 2004. The offices of the radio station HAPY FM 108.3. RICK *Deltoro, a white, middle-aged radio DJ, is in the broadcast room, a swing microphone and some notes in front of him. He's on the air.* CHILI, *his young producer, is in the control booth. They are separated by a large window.*

RICK: That was TLC, "Waterfalls," on 108.3 HAPY FM. And speaking of waterfalls. . .

He laughs.

That's the worst. That's the worst segue in, like, the *history* of radio.

He laughs; CHILI *laughs.*

This thing, this disaster in—all over—in Southeast Asia, it's been a couple of days and the death toll is just. . . it's like watching *The English Patient*, you think it's gotta be over, but it just *keeps going*, it's—awful, really, it's truly awful.

CHILI: The movie, *and* the—

CHILI *laughs.*

RICK: No, no. . . it's bad, Chili, it's bad.

CHILI: Oh, totally, totally—

RICK: And we should—everyone—should be, like, just go there. People oughta just *go there*. Build homes or something, do *something*, don't just sit on your ass and watch it on TV, or—

CHILI: Well, people have jobs; they can't just—

RICK: That's not the point—

CHILI: We should send the unemployed—y'know what, send the homeless! We should all—every country should just send their homeless people, to build—

RICK: No, no, that's—*(laughs) for* the homeless *by* the homeless—no, obviously, that's a terrible idea.

Anyway, anyway. So. . . there's a lot of fundraising going on, for relief, and I got this email—did you get this, Chil? It's a *contest*. Coca-Cola is holding this raffle contest thing to go *live* in Sri Lanka, in this coastal town, it's totally free; they just *give* it to you—

CHILI: What, now?

RICK: No, not *now*, there's dead Sri Lankans everywhere—that'd be the worst contest ever—well, it's *already*, I think, the worst contest—you go in four years.

CHILI: Oh, I *did* hear about this. It's the "big backyard" something.

RICK: "The world's biggest backyard contest," yah.

CHILI: They're gonna rebuild the town, right?

RICK: Yah, it's all underwritten by USAID, the American, whatever, relief, whatever; they fix it all up, takes about four years, and then the winner goes and lives there in this giant house—

CHILI: I would totally go, *totally*, that's amazing.

RICK: Are you on friggin' acid? What's the matter with you?

CHILI: Like *you* wouldn't want—

RICK: You know what it is? You know what it is?

CHILI: What is it?

RICK: It's *sponsored* colonialism. That's what it is. It's the Americans—

CHILI: It's a fundraiser! For relief, they *need* that over there.

RICK: You're an idiot.

CHILI: I'm not saying you should—

RICK: Seriously, how do you not swallow your own tongue? Okay, okay, I'll break it down for you like you're a first-grader. . .

There is a knock at the door. SANJAY *is outside.*

Oh my god, it's Jian Ghomeshi!

RICK *and* CHILI *laugh.* RICK *waves* SANJAY *inside.*

No, no, sorry, that's just Sanjay. Come on in. Sanjay works upstairs. Grab a seat, buddy.

He does.

Sanjay, what do you think about this stupid Coca-Cola contest?

SANJAY: *(a bit of a deer in headlights)* Uh. . . well, it's—

RICK: Sanjay's with corporate, he probably likes the idea.

CHILI: He's mad he didn't think of it first.

SANJAY: No, I think it's. . . well, it's a complex. . .

RICK: Sanjay, you know this is radio, right? You have to speak in complete sentences in radio.

SANJAY: I think Coke is actually a sponsor, so. . .

RICK: *(laughing)* Oh my God, you are such a suit. Okay, okay, I'm gonna throw to a commercial. Maybe a Coke commercial, who knows? We'll be back with more of Toronto's top music on HAPY 108.3.

He hits a button and we hear the 108.3 jingle.

CHILI: Rick, you want me in there for—

RICK: Shut the fuck up.

RICK presses a button to silence CHILI, looks at SANJAY.

Never knock at the door when I'm on-air.

SANJAY: Sorry.

RICK glares.

I think it's good.

RICK: What?

SANJAY: The contest. I think it's a good idea. USAID is a. . . they do good work.

RICK: There's some serious fucking devastation going on and it's being *trivialized* by this. . . y'know how much USAID contributes to sustainability in foreign development? Nothing. They contract everything out, create a market for American—it's bullshit, it's all bullshit. You know what Cuntoleezza Rice said about what's going on over there? She said it's a "wonderful opportunity" that will reap "great dividends" for the US. It's a fucking travesty.

What do you want?

Beat.

SANJAY: Rough morning?

RICK: They're all rough, these mornings.

SANJAY: I've got some notes, from upstairs.

RICK: I'm halfway done the show already!

SANJAY: They're a bit late, yah.

RICK: Am I the only one around here that does his fucking job properly?

SANJAY: It's not my fault, they—

RICK: I'll decide what's your fault.

Threatening beat.

SANJAY: The notes are. . . they're tiny, really, most of them are positive. They love the game show bit, and the Osama prank call; they think the demo will love it. Focus groups are really digging the relationship with you and Chili; they think he's great.

SANJAY gives CHILI the thumbs-up.

RICK: Yah, he can't hear us.

SANJAY: Oh. Well, in that case, they didn't really say that; they're actually thinking of bringing in a third person to pick up the slack. There's just one minor thing. . . *(like ripping off a Band-Aid)* unfortunately, you don't have clearance for the song.

RICK: Fuckin' *knew it.*

SANJAY: *(throws up his hands)* It's a rights issue, we can't—

RICK: There's no "rights issue."

SANJAY: It's a *management* issue.

RICK: It's a *censorship* issue.

SANJAY: No, no, look, they love it, love the concept—think it's brilliant, it's just a logistical—

RICK: Fuck you. You're handling me.

Beat.

SANJAY: Okay. I'm handling you.

RICK: *(surprised, and a little impressed)* All right, finally, some real talk.

CHILI's voice cuts in from the control booth.

CHILI: Rick, you're back on-air in three. . . two. . .

RICK doesn't break eye contact with SANJAY. He swings the microphone over to him and hits a button.

RICK: I'm in the middle of something, here's some more mind-numbing pop music.

He hits the button again and swings the microphone away. Back to SANJAY.

Tell me what they said.

Beat.

SANJAY: They hate the song.

RICK: There it is.

SANJAY: They think it's insensitive.

RICK: It's a comedy show. They know it's a *comedy* show, right?

SANJAY: They do, Rick.

RICK: This is why they hired me; they *hired* me because—in their words—they liked my "edge." I'm "edgy." That's why.

SANJAY: They just think. . . maybe it's too soon.

RICK: That's why it's called *current* affairs.

SANJAY: They don't want to take it lightly.

RICK: It's got nothing to do with taking it lightly!

   RICK *stews in the frustration of being misunderstood.*

What do you think?

SANJAY: Me?

RICK: What do you think of the song?

SANJAY: I haven't heard it.

RICK: You haven't heard it.

SANJAY: I'm not in those meetings.

RICK: You haven't heard it.

SANJAY: It's the principle.

RICK: The "principle"?

SANJAY: I understand that humour is. . . that some people deal with some situations that way. But not everyone is like that. And not every situation is. . . well, *appropriate*, for that treatment. It's like making a joke about 9/11.

RICK: Well, you know what they say about 9/11 jokes: They're just *plane* wrong.

> *Beat.* SANJAY *laughs, despite himself.*

You see?!? It's funny! Wait, are you laughing 'cause it's funny, or 'cause you're a terrorist?

SANJAY: Hey. . .

RICK: I'm kidding! And I know 9/11 itself isn't *actually* funny, but maybe the *reverence* that we give it. . . maybe we can laugh about that, just a little.

SANJAY: I guess. . . but, look, I can't let you do it. They sent me down to make sure you *don't* do it. I'm just being straight with you.

RICK: What, you're my babysitter now?

SANJAY: I'm just—I'm a representative of the corporate entity—

RICK: Babysitter. They gave you the bitch job, coming down here; what'd you do, fuck someone's wife? Daughter? Gerbil? What?

SANJAY: I volunteered.

RICK: No one *volunteers* to come into the shark tank, baby.

SANJAY: I'm a fan, Rick.

RICK gives him the finger.

It's true. I love the show. I'm the biggest supporter you've got upstairs. I'm fighting for you, but you gotta meet them halfway. They don't want you to make fun of this.

RICK: I'm not making fun of—it's our *reaction* to it. The song I want to do. . . it's a parody of those fucking useless charity songs. You know the ones? No, you're probably not old enough to. . . Back in '84 Bob Geldof recorded "Do They Know It's Christmas?" with this supergroup of all-stars like Bono and Bananarama called Band Aid, for African famine relief. Then in '85, Quincy Jones did his own version, same deal, called USA for Africa.

SANJAY: "We Are the World."

RICK: Right. A week after they recorded that, David fucking Foster gets all these Canadian assholes to do "Tears Are Not Enough." Northern Lights they called it.

SANJAY: And you think those songs are useless.

RICK: You think some starving African is gonna be like, "Oh. . . fuckin'. . . Burton Cummings is singing about me, the world's a better place." They don't care! It's a *vanity* project; all three of them are vanity projects. Morrissey called Band Aid "the most self-righteous platform ever in the history of popular music." And Morrissey is a fucking asshole!

SANJAY: But those songs. . . they did a lot for famine relief. To raise awareness, and the profits from the album sales, individual donations to—

RICK: In 1985, sure, fine. But in 2004? Gimme a fucking break. Album sales are in the toilet, awareness is. . . No one cares. We've saturated them with this gooey, saccharine, bullshit marketing. . . everyone just nods their heads and waits for fucking Bono and George Clooney to cure AIDS—I'm fucking sick of it!

CHILI's voice cuts in again.

CHILI: You're back in three, two. . .

RICK repeats the business with the microphone, swinging it over and hitting the button.

RICK: I AM FUCKING *TALKING!*

Swings it away. Beat. They all slowly realize what happened.

SANJAY: You just said the F-word on live radio.

RICK: It's fine, there's a delay. Chili caught that, didn't you?

CHILI: Nope. You told me to take the delay off last week, said it was blocking your chi.

SANJAY: You're out of control—

RICK: Whatever, I doubt anyone heard that.

CHILI: Rick, Barry is on the line from upstairs, he wants to know why you just swore on live radio.

SANJAY: Jesus Christ, I'm gonna get fired. I'm supposed to be *watching* you!

RICK picks up the phone.

RICK: Hey, Barry—

He rips the phone cord out of the wall, throws the lifeless phone on the ground.

(to SANJAY) The problem with producers and—in particular— producers of comedy shows. . . is that most of them, they see a joke as a position. That if you tell a joke about something, then that must mean it's how you feel, the *position* you take, and that you are *defending* that position by telling the joke. But that's wrong. That's wrong because a joke isn't a position, a joke is a *proposition*. It's an invitation that I leave up there, hanging in the air; it's for the *listener*, the *receiver* to do something with it.

SANJAY: What if it's too far, though?

RICK: Y'know, guys like Lenny Bruce and Richard Pryor, they were crucified for saying the hard things, the hard words that woke us up. Shook us out of apathy. Revealed to us the fucking hypocrisy and the unfairness and the. . . you know what I'm talking about?

SANJAY: This isn't pirate radio, it's a commercial broadcast; we're accountable to people: regulatory bodies, sponsors. . . there are checks and balances—

RICK: Those corporate pussies care more about money and focus groups than they do about the right thing! The greater good! And you're better than that, we both are. I do this song, this song I'm not cleared to do, and I *will* change things. I *will* get people talking about what's happening over there. We have the ears of hundreds of thousands of people. . . *that's* the accountability I care about.

SANJAY: It's my job, Rick. All I've got is my job.

Beat. RICK *looks at* SANJAY *carefully.*

RICK: Sanjay, we are at a. . . critical. . . time. We've become so fucking apathetic. . . something like this happens and it's "that thing that happened *over there*. To *those people*." So they have a vigil, a charity concert, a fucking *contest*. . . all those things, they do more to separate *us* from *them* than they do to help. I'm trying to get people to care again. And I'm doing it through comedy, because that's my gift. That's my jam. And I feel like you get that.

You're a fan of the show? How'd you like to be *on* the show? You, me and Chili, the three muske-fucking-teers. Stand with me today and I will make that happen. I want you to be a part of this, but it's gotta be now.

Beat. SANJAY *thinks.*

CHILI: Rick, they're sending security down; they're gonna pull us and throw to requests, are we gonna do this thing?

RICK: *(to* SANJAY*)* Are we doing this?

Beat.

SANJAY: Do it.

RICK: *(smiles)* Lock that door.

> SANJAY *locks the door.* RICK *sits down at the desk, pulls the microphone over and speaks to* CHILI.

Cue up the David Foster segment for backup.

This is activism, Sanjay, real talk. This is a protest song. I'm like Bob Marley up in this bitch. Or like a funnier Gandhi.

There is banging at the studio door.

SANJAY: They're here.

RICK: We're making a difference. *You're* making a difference. Here we go.

He hits a button.

Good morning, Toronto. I got Sanjay here in the studio with me, Chili in the booth and the whole twenty-eighth floor kicking down our door because *everyone* wants to hear "The Tsunami Song," a heartfelt tribute to accompany the images of poor brown people being washed away on the front page of your newspaper. Unless you read the *Sun,* where the front page is a blond with big tits and daddy issues on a waterslide. Almost the same thing. Chili, you ready?

The backing track starts playing, to the tune of "Tears Are Not Enough."

This one's for my man Sanjay.

RICK *sings. Maybe* CHILI *backs him up.*

Every single day
There's thousands of earthquakes
But we don't care 'cause it's not us

They're half a world away
With names that we can't say
Just more dead foreigners, so what?

But then there came a wave
Washed the Asian kids away
Now it's just empty, wet sweatshops

Your mommy tried to swim
But she got her head caved in
Bet you have questions for your God

You gave me cat, I ordered chicken
You're hanging on to Communism
The tsunami came because God hates you all

Because you ate your dog for dinner
Drowned your baby girl in the Yangtze River
The tsunami came because God hates you all

 Beat. SANJAY *is horrified.* RICK *is self-satisfied.*

Next up, traffic and weather together on the ones, 108.3 HAPY FM.

 RICK *removes the headphones, smiles up at* SANJAY.

S'funny, right?

SANJAY unlocks the door to the studio. It bursts open, men grab RICK and pull him out of the studio. SANJAY stands, staring after him, unable to say anything.

THE ORPHAN BOY STORY

Bandaranaike International Airport, Sri Lanka. January 1, 2005. THE HARD-BOILED MAN, *an older Chinese man, enters with* KID, *a young girl of about six. He is uncomfortable around her. She is uncomfortable around him. They are both dressed in other people's clothes, found clothes from dead people's suitcases. He checks the boards for the arrival times. He gestures for* KID *to sit. She is defiant. They have a staring contest. He wins; she sits. He sits down next to her. She gets up and moves several seats over. He lets it go. He tries to read a book, keeping an eye on her. If someone gets too close, he stares them down. If she talks to anyone, he orders her to be quiet. He is a guard dog, a Rottweiler-man. They sit for a long time in silence. An announcement comes over the PA announcing a flight arriving from Kuala Lumpur. He feels the need to say something.*

THE HARD-BOILED MAN: Hey.

No response.

Hey.

No response.

(in harsh Cantonese) Wei.

She looks over. He doesn't actually know what to say.

Hungry?

KID: No.

He slides over a chocolate bar.

THE HARD-BOILED MAN: Eat.

She slides it back at him. She takes out a picture of her parents, stares at it longingly. A long silence.

THE HARD-BOILED MAN doesn't know what to say. He is out of his depth. He growls. More silence. Then:

My parents are dead, too.

She looks over, briefly, then goes back to what she was doing. He talks so she can hear, but mainly to himself.

A long time ago. I was your age. A little older, maybe.

It was hard.

Beat.

Don't listen to the other kids. They don't understand. They'll. . . they'll make fun of you. They made fun of me.

Beat.

One boy. Kai. . . something. He was younger, but I was small. He was a bully, in my school.

Beat.

The bully. . . he called me an orphan, in front of all the other boys. He did this. . . every day. The Orphan Boy, that's what he called me. And he would laugh, him and his brother.

Beat. KID *is starting to pay attention.*

But that summer, I grew tall. Taller than the bully. So the next fall term, I marched up to him in the schoolyard, first thing in the morning. I stood in front of him, and I asked him, "What's my name?". . . and before he could answer, I punched him in the nose.

He punches his hand, to illustrate.

I broke it.

He looks at KID.

Do you know how to break someone's nose?

She shakes her head in wonder.

Don't punch them straight on, here.

He indicates the tip of his nose.

You want to aim *here (indicating the side of the nasal bridge)* and *down*. It's a clean break. Easy to fix. But they'll never forget you. And they'll never call you an orphan again.

Beat. She considers this. She punches her hand, imitating him. He nods.

Good.

The PA announces a flight landing from Hong Kong. That's the flight they've been waiting for. THE HARD-BOILED MAN *stands up and so does* KID. *They look over at the arrivals gate.*

You watch and tell me which one is your uncle, okay? He said to meet him here.

They wait. THE HARD-BOILED MAN *wants to put his hand on* KID's *shoulder, but he can't bring himself to. They stand awkwardly, together yet apart. Finally, he takes*

*a receipt from his pocket and writes something on it.
He grunts at* KID, *who looks up at him. He gives her
the paper.*

That's my phone number. In London, that's where I live now.

She puts it in her pocket, not sure what else to do. Beat.

Life is going to be hard. For you. So. . . you can call me. If you
ever. . .

    Beat.

You don't know me. And I don't know you. You're just a kid.
And it's not the same as having your parents, I'm not that, to
you. . . I'm just. . .

    Beat.

I'm the one who pulled you out of the water.

And you can call me.

If you need that.

Again.

    Beat. A man walks towards them. KID *starts at the sight
of him.*

56

Is that?

KID: Yi suk suk! *[Uncle!]*

> *She runs towards him.* THE HARD-BOILED MAN *watches carefully as she rushes to embrace her uncle, who bends down to hold her. After a moment, the uncle looks up and sees* THE HARD-BOILED MAN. *A look of recognition crosses his face.* THE HARD-BOILED MAN *recognizes him, too, a foggy memory at first, then becoming clearer.*

THE HARD-BOILED MAN: You. . .

> *The man stands up, slowly, eyes locked on* THE HARD-BOILED MAN. *His hand reaches up in reflex, touching his long-ago broken nose. He wraps his arm around* KID *to protect her.*

> THE HARD-BOILED MAN *looks down, averting the man's gaze. He turns his back to them and walks away.* KID *and her uncle walk away as well, but* KID *breaks away and runs to* THE HARD-BOILED MAN. *She catches him and wraps herself around his leg in a giant hug.* THE HARD-BOILED MAN *doesn't know what to do. He looks down at her, still hugging his leg.*

Okay.

> *She lets go of his leg and smiles up at him. She goes back to her uncle, and they make their way off.*

THE HARD-BOILED MAN *watches them go. He manages something reminiscent of a smile.*

Okay.

He leaves the airport.

THE WATER STORY

*Khao Lak, Thailand. Darkness. The sound of sex.
Rushed for him. Languid for her. Waves crashing against
her shore. A climax. Then another. A sacred pause.*

*Lights. A hotel room. A sprawl of limbs on the bed sep-
arates into two people.* JASMINE *is Thai; pristine, slender
and petite.* CRUMB *is the opposite of her. He is burdened
and white and rather asexual. They are both naked,
thinly coated in sweat.* CRUMB *breathes heavily, this is
the most he's worked out in years.* JASMINE *is composed,
always. She rises, still naked, goes to the vanity and
lights a long cigarette.* CRUMB *watches her, intent. She
smokes, draped over the vanity chair, on display for him.*

CRUMB: Look at you. Made for this, weren't you? Built for this.
To do this.

She smiles coyly, still on the clock.

When he said you were the one, the special one, one with. . . talent. . . he wasn't kidding. I mean, he's a lot of things, but a liar ain't one of 'em. You're a lot of things too, but a liar-maker you are not.

Beat.

Jesus. I mean, sorry, are you religious?—but, c'mon, *Jesus.* That was intense.

Did you. . . I mean. . . I know you. . . there was a sound, and you did that thing, but. . . and you're supposed to, aren't you? Isn't that part of the "contract" or whatever it is, to. . . I just want to know. Was that real?

She opens her mouth to speak.

No, second thought, don't tell me. I don't want to know. I mean, that's why, y'know, we pay. We pay for the—for the right, for the *privilege*. . . not to know. To assume. The, uh. . .

JASMINE: *(draws the word out)* fantasy.

CRUMB: Lie.

JASMINE raises an eyebrow.

Fantasy. Sure. Why not.

Beat.

JASMINE: may i dress?

CRUMB: *(an attempt at being coy)* If you like.

She begins to dress.

But only just. Okay?

He nods towards her lingerie.

Only those.

JASMINE: as you like.

She puts her underwear on at the same rhythm you would imagine she undressed. The act never lets up.

CRUMB: Man, I am sweating. The heat here. . .

JASMINE: it comes in waves.

CRUMB: It's different. From, you know, at home. . . it's different. There are seasons back home.

Not here. No seasons here.

Beat.

My wife. She didn't like the seasons. It was too much change. She liked the warm. Warm and hot. Those were her seasons. She used to say. . .

Beat. He shuts up.

Sorry.

JASMINE: you can tell me about her. i won't mind.

CRUMB: I know.

JASMINE: mr. crumb. . . our friend connected us because I have certain skills. certain talents that you were. . . in *need* of. listening. . . is one of those talents.

Beat.

CRUMB: That thing you did with your tongue. That's a talent. Listening is just what you do when you ain't got nothing to say.

JASMINE: i am not some pattaya bar girl, mr. crumb. my time is precious. you would be wise not to waste it. or you might find it running out.

She begins to dress further.

CRUMB: I'm sorry. Don't. . . look, don't go. Okay? I just. . . please don't go.

She halts.

I've got a lot on my mind is all. Sex. . . does that to me. It makes everything hazy, confused. That's why I like it. I used to drink. You know? A lot. But I prefer sex. Helps with the forgetting. The disappearance of fact. You know? So I'm sorry. I didn't mean. . . I can be brash; I know that. I'm sorry.

Beat.

Let's have a drink.

He gets some glasses and tiny bottles from the mini-bar.

JASMINE: i thought you didn't drink anymore.

CRUMB: Don't think I forgot how.

JASMINE: but you used to be sober.

CRUMB: I used to be a lot of things.

JASMINE: *(an attempt to lighten the mood)* would you like to play a game?

CRUMB: Like a drinking game? Little old for that, aren't I? Not you, maybe, but I certainly am.

JASMINE: if you can guess my drink, we'll add another hour. gratis.

CRUMB: Heh.

Beat.

Two hours.

JASMINE: *(smiles)* as you like.

> CRUMB *studies her. He pours himself a Jack and Coke,*
> *stirs it thoughtfully and ponders her.*

CRUMB: Something classy. Sophisticated. You're not a Jack and Coke, that's me. But you're not one a'them—whatsit-called—"crantini" ladies, are you? No. Nothing that takes too much time. Can't be bothered shaking and stirring when you're on someone else's dime. Simple. But refined. Standard, so you can get it room to room, bar to bar. . . quality changes but the drink's always there.

> *He analyzes the mini-bar choices.*

Heh.

> *He produces a bottle of spring water and tosses it to her.*

That's it, isn't it?

JASMINE: very clever of you.

> *She sets the water aside.*

but it's gin soda.

CRUMB: Oh.

JASMINE: you were right about everything else.

CRUMB: Sure.

JASMINE: don't be upset.

CRUMB: I'm not upset. Just a stupid game, is all. I don't get upset over stupid games.

JASMINE: interesting choice. water.

CRUMB: You mentioned that.

JASMINE: i mentioned it was "clever." "clever". . . is not always "interesting."

CRUMB: You speak like a sphinx.

JASMINE: i like you, mr. crumb. you are a decidedly non-evil man. and i appreciate that in a person. i can't always say that.

He slides her a glass.

CRUMB: Your gin soda.

Beat.

What is this like? This business, for you? I mean, is it rewarding? Do you. . . have you. . . the people, I mean. . . what am I asking? *(a breath)* Have you found love, Jasmine? Do you know what "love" is?

JASMINE: must i?

CRUMB: Suppose not. Must help, though, I'd think. To know what that is. S'like your competition, isn't it? You should know your competition. That thing that you fight against, that—what, that—threatens you. Your existence. Isn't love that thing?

JASMINE: i have an arrhythmia in my heart. love aggravates it. it's no more a competition than happiness would be. i am never wanting for love. never starved for it. it's everywhere around me. in you, even. i just can't get too close. my heart wouldn't take that.

CRUMB: You got the nicest way of saying the saddest things.

JASMINE: thank you.

CRUMB: So then what do you get outta this? Things like this?

> JASMINE *takes an envelope full of cash from the vanity. Her payment. She takes a few bills out and rubs them over her body.*

JASMINE: *(imitating a Pattaya bar girl)* money, baby. . .

CRUMB: Oh yah? That's what it's all about for you?

She drops the act, and the bills, to the floor.

JASMINE: that's what you foreigners believe. shame, mr. crumb, I thought you were a rarer breed of man than that.

CRUMB: S'why I was asking. I don't believe that about you. I don't believe it's money. You're different. . .

JASMINE: don't romanticize me, mr. crumb, it never ends well for either party.

CRUMB: I'm just curious.

JASMINE: as am i. how a man like you resolves to find someone like me.

CRUMB: Lots'a men here looking for girls. . .

JASMINE: but only extraordinary men look for me. so what makes you extraordinary?

CRUMB: I'm gettin' tired of your questions, lady.

JASMINE: i mean no offence.

CRUMB: I'm tired all the same.

He pours himself another Jack and Coke and starts to dress.

Questions, right? You can't just ask people their lives, lady. You gotta respect people's boundaries, or somethin'. Can't go askin' them about things, their motivating *things*, you understand? We get nervous, people do, when we're called into question like that.

JASMINE: and sometimes a question is just a question. nothing more.

CRUMB: There's always more.

> *Beat. The direction of this conversation has thrown him.*
> *He is as insecure as a boy.*

I want to know if it was real. When you came, just then, was that real? I can't. . . I can't stand being lied to. I want to know if it was real. Tell me.

JASMINE: why does it matter to you?

CRUMB: Just answer my question. . .

JASMINE: mr. crumb—

CRUMB: Stop calling me that, okay!? Okay? It's not my real name; my name isn't "Mr. Crumb," just stop calling me that.

> *Pause.*

JASMINE: what did you used to be called?

Beat.

CRUMB: "Sharky." She used to. . . 'cause we met on this beach, and I was doing the *Jaws* thing for my nephew; you know the. . .

He puts his hand on his head like a fin.

. . .under the water. She saw me do that and she knew she was going to fall in love. So she called me Sharky. Or. . . Thomas. Sometimes just Thomas.

JASMINE: i could call you that.

He quickly finishes his drink and fumbles with another.

CRUMB: Why do you ask me these things? Make me remember these things, why do you do that?

JASMINE: why do you want to forget?

CRUMB: I don't. I wasn't saying that. . .

JASMINE: so tell me.

CRUMB: She was kind. Y'know?

She never said a bad thing about anybody. Always looked for the best—but when she was disappointed in you. . . boy, you knew it. And she loved the water. That was a thing.

She loved. . .

He breaks a bit. There's a beat. He recovers.

The sex was good. Not often, but good when it happened. She
never came, though. We got close a few times; she thought she
was. . . I guess there's, like a brink that you get to. And you either
give in to it, or you get scared of it and you pull back.

Beat. A quiet laugh.

There was one time she tried to fake it. Just as I was ready she
started—on top of me, riding me—she started to moan real
loud. She starts grinding harder, faster, and this moaning. . . I
totally buy it, and then she starts talking, right? Dirty, like. She's
going, "Yah, give it to me, do it like that," and all this stuff,
'cause I told her I liked that this real long time ago, but she was
never the sort. So now she's going like a house on fire and I'm
thinking *something really fucking cool has come over my wife*.
She's possessed, this beautiful tornado of a thing, and I'm still
buying it. So she's screaming all this stuff, and I'm praying to
God to hold on long enough to get her there, and then she stops,
she draws herself in real deep and real close, grabs my face in
her hands and says, "Oh, baby, take me to that special place."

Beat.

I lose it. I start laughing. I mean, who says that? I'm dying of
laughter, and she—there's this look she gets—but then she's
laughing too. We're both killing ourselves and she falls down

on top'a me. . . she couldn't fake a smile, my love couldn't. She was something special.

Beat.

I was supposed to meet her here, New Year's Day. I had this work thing, I couldn't. . . but she went ahead. I told her to go ahead. *I'll meet you there. We'll have our anniversary in the sand.* Our anniversary. Would'a been our first anniversary.

New Year's Day. Someone found her. . . uh, her necklace. This Celtic knot thing. It was fucking ugly but she loved it. Never took it off, y'know? That's how we. . . I guess, how I knew. Our anniversary. It was the first day I took someone home. I paid someone to come home with me.

Beat.

Couldn't do it, y'know? Couldn't face the— *(He starts to break.)* I made her wear the necklace. I dressed her up in. . . in her favourite—fuck, her favourite dress—from home, I put it on her. I smothered her neck in perfume and I—Jesus—I told her not to come. I told her to get to the brink, but don't go over, don't you fucking go over. Oh fuck. It was good, too. It was so--oh, God. . .

CRUMB *hangs his face in his hands.* JASMINE *sits next to him on the bed. They don't touch. She isn't awkward or uneasy, just there. They say nothing for a long while.*

Draw me a bath, would ya?

71

JASMINE: sure.

She goes to the bathtub and runs the water. The tub starts filling up.

CRUMB: This place swallowed her. I tried to swallow it back, but there's too damn much.

JASMINE: is that why you're here?

CRUMB: You know why I'm here.

I need help. I can't do it alone.

JASMINE: why did you let me come? you could've stopped me. kept me at the brink.

CRUMB: Things change.

JASMINE: do you want me to tell you if it was real?

Beat.

CRUMB: No. No, I don't think I do.

He begins to get undressed. She helps him until he is standing, naked, in front of the bath.

You'll stay?

JASMINE: it is our arrangement.

He gets in the bath. He lets the water from the tap run down his face, matting his hair.

CRUMB: What does it feel like? I mean, real or not, with me, I don't care. . . but you have, haven't you? With someone?

JASMINE: i have.

CRUMB: What does it feel like? What's on the other side that she was so afraid to see?

Beat.

JASMINE: it feels. . . it feels like you're being carried away on the crest of a wave. and it might set you down gentle and it might set you down rough. . . but you never feel that. i promise you, sharky, you never feel that. all you ever feel is being carried away. out and away.

Beat. CRUMB *exhales all the air in his body. He smiles.*

CRUMB: Oh, baby. Take me to that special place.

He disappears under the water. Quiet. JASMINE *sits on the bed. The water gets rough.* CRUMB's *legs start kicking, short and sharp jerks.* CRUMB's *palm comes over the side of the tub and grips it hard. Against his will, his face breaks the surface of the water. He curses. Sputters and coughs. Tries again, disappearing under the water. It gets rough, and again he resurfaces against his will. He looks at* JASMINE. *She can't look back. He takes her hand gently and places it on his chest. He disappears under the water again. Struggles.* JASMINE's *arm goes rigid, holding him under. Her eyes burn. Moments pass. The water goes still. Beat.* JASMINE *gets up, dresses, moves to the door. She picks up the envelope with her payment in it. She takes the money out and finds a silver Celtic knot necklace inside. She considers this, then replaces all the contents, money and necklace, back in the envelope. Sets it back down on the vanity. She leaves the room.*

THE FALLING STORY

Somewhere beneath the ground. KINTARO *Kobayashi is falling down a hole. Air rushes by him. He begins to nod off. He tries to fight it, but eventually he falls asleep. After a beat, another man—*MAKOTO *Aoki—falls past him. As he passes he calls out, Doppler-like...*

MAKOTO: Kobayashi-saaaaanaaaaaaaan. . . . .

KINTARO *wakes up. He looks around. No one.*

KINTARO: Strange.

He goes back to sleep. Another beat, and MAKOTO *floats back up, spread out like a leaf on the wind. He is wearing a skydiving suit and has a belt with a rope attached that runs upwards. He floats next to* KINTARO.

MAKOTO: Kobayashi-san?

KINTARO *wakes up.*

KINTARO: What's going on?

MAKOTO: I can't believe I found you.

KINTARO: Who are you?

MAKOTO: Makoto Aoki.

KINTARO: You don't look Japanese.

MAKOTO: I am from the north.

KINTARO: *I* am from the north.

MAKOTO: I am from the *far* north.

KINTARO: I don't know you. Do I?

MAKOTO: You do not. What do you remember?

KINTARO: I fell down a hole.

MAKOTO: Yes.

KINTARO: I'm. . . still. . . falling down a hole.

MAKOTO: Yes.

KINTARO: I thought I was dead. Am I dead?

MAKOTO: No. You are falling down a hole. When you die, you wake up on the subway.

KINTARO: That's absurd.

MAKOTO: And yet, here we are.

KINTARO: How long have I been gone?

MAKOTO: That may be difficult to—

KINTARO: Please, I have no patience for—

MAKOTO: You've been gone four and a half years.

> *Beat.*

KINTARO: That's a long time.

MAKOTO: It is.

KINTARO: How deep is this hole?

MAKOTO: I don't know. I would have to say it is at least four and a half years deep. Maybe five.

KINTARO: Imagine that. . . How did you find me?

MAKOTO: I have a knowledge of holes.

KINTARO: You are vaguer than a dimly lit room.

MAKOTO: Kobayashi-san, I will answer your questions. . . and then I have one for you. An important question that I have submitted myself down here to be answered. But my story begins with you and how you found yourself in this hole.

KINTARO: You don't know?

MAKOTO: I have my ideas. The last anyone heard from you, you were in India. They had just identified your. . . your daughter's remains. After that, it was a mystery as to where you went.

Beat.

KINTARO: Toronto. I went to Toronto.

MAKOTO: To her apartment.

KINTARO: Hai. When I arrived there. . . I thought I was in the wrong place. Mess everywhere. Bits of foil and syringes for drugs. The girl that lived in that place was a dark version of the daughter I knew. The same on the outside, but frightening inside.

MAKOTO: I was afraid you had seen this. . .

KINTARO: I was. . . despondent. . . I turned on a radio for some music; I find music soothing. But this station. . . they were playing a song, a song I recognized, but the words were. . . twisted. Cruel. Impossibly cruel. I took a step backwards, and that's when it happened. I heard a floorboard crack and I fell. Down a hole. I don't know where it came from. I guess it had been hiding there, under the floor.

Beat.

MAKOTO: And the hole did not. . . speak. . . to you?

KINTARO: Certainly not. It's a hole, what would it say?

MAKOTO: Hai. And, Kobayashi-san, can you tell me. . . how did you not starve?

KINTARO: Every now and again, when I get hungry, a chicken salad sandwich falls down the hole.

Followed by a bottle of water, or orange juice. Sometimes I feel like I'm trapped in the bottom of a vending machine in Kyoto, you know the ones.

MAKOTO: Fascinating. Kobayashi-san, there is a deli down the street from me, and a little while ago I noticed the owner throwing a chicken salad sandwich into a small hole near the back of the kitchen. That's what gave me hope you were still alive.

KINTARO: You'd think I'd get tired of chicken salad sandwiches after four and a half years, but they're quite delicious.

MAKOTO: Yes, I eat there often. The secret is cumin.

KINTARO: But I wasn't in a deli at the time, I was in Alice's apartment.

MAKOTO: They must be connected, the holes.

KINTARO: I'm having a hard time believing any of this. You are full of fantastic statements, young man. I demand you tell me what's happening. Who are you, how do you know my name?

MAKOTO: The truth is, Kobayashi-san, I knew your daughter. We were lovers for a short time. She was outrageously beautiful and, as you can see, I am quite ordinary. But we fell in love, nonetheless.

KINTARO: Impossible. I've never even heard your name.

MAKOTO: But I have heard yours. One day, Alice was out and I was alone in her apartment. I was standing by the radio, in the same place you stood, and I heard a noise beneath me. Like the sound in an airplane cabin, air being forced through a vent or turbine. . . I obsessed about it, finally prying up the floorboard to look. And that's when I first saw the hole. "That's strange," I said. And, to my surprise, the hole answered back, "Not really."

KINTARO: The hole spoke to you?

MAKOTO: I thought maybe I was crazy, but the hole kept talking to me. We had a lengthy and rather involved conversation about Kafka, of all things.

KINTARO: This is absurd. You can't expect me to believe—

MAKOTO: I asked the hole what it was doing there, in Alice's apartment, and it said it was waiting. . . it was waiting for Kobayashi Kintaro. Not Alice. Not me. The hole was waiting for you. I asked it why. It said, "Why is a hole in the ground a hole in the ground? Is it the absence of something beneath it, or is it the very purpose for it being there to begin with?" I don't know the answer.

Beat. KINTARO *thinks.*

When you disappeared, I knew the hole must have found you. I've been living above you for these four and a half years. Sometimes I play music, Brahms or Bach, mostly. Sometimes a Tchaikovsky, if I'm feeling in a mood.

KINTARO: There *was* music. . . hah. I thought I was going mad.

MAKOTO: The hole hadn't spoken to me the entire time I've lived above you. Except today. Today it said something and it's why I've come to find you.

KINTARO: What did it say?

MAKOTO: It said, simply: "Someone else needs this hole, now."

Beat.

KINTARO: You had a question. You told me, earlier. An important question.

MAKOTO: You've already answered it.

Short beat. KINTARO *doesn't understand.*

When I told you who I was. . . you said you'd never heard of me. Not my name, or. . . she never spoke of me, did she?

KINTARO *shakes his head.*

Your Alice, my Alice. . . maybe these things are not connected. Not like the holes in the apartment and the deli. Maybe our Alices were different after all.

Beat.

KINTARO: Maybe. . .

MAKOTO: Yes?

KINTARO: Our last vacation together. We were in Italy.

MAKOTO: I remember. Vatican City was her favourite.

KINTARO: During the trip. . . she had on a ring. Never took it off. Silver, a simple ring.

MAKOTO: Yes. I gave that to her.

KINTARO: She would turn it around and around when we were walking. Smiling when she did, and thinking. Maybe of you.

Beat. MAKOTO *smiles at this.*

Do you miss her?

MAKOTO: When I heard. . . my heart turned to dust. I coughed, and my heart scattered out in the wind, never to be seen again.

KINTARO: Hm.

Beat.

MAKOTO: I have a rope. It is attached to a winch that is bolted to the floor in her apartment. If I press this button it will pull us up.

KINTARO: That's a long rope.

MAKOTO: It is about four and a half years long.

KINTARO: Just in time, then.

MAKOTO: Just in time.

Beat.

KINTARO: Maybe. . .

MAKOTO: Yes?

KINTARO: This hole is the last thing I have of her. And it's. . . well, it's a hole. I know it sounds. . . but maybe just one more day. I'm not done falling down yet.

MAKOTO: *(nods his acquiescence)* I will buy more rope.

KINTARO: Domo.

MAKOTO: *(bows as well as he can while falling down a hole)* Do itashi mashite.

> MAKOTO *pushes a button and begins moving upwards. When he is gone,* KINTARO *takes a deep breath. He hugs the air around him.*

KINTARO: Sabishii desu. . .

> *He continues falling.*

THE MILLIMETRE STORY

Salt Lake City, Utah, 2009. LENORE *is packing a bag. She is an Asian woman in her mid-thirties. Her house is in disarray, boxes everywhere, and plastic tarps hang over furniture. The only part untouched is the kitchen, where she has been baking a pie. There is a knock at the door. She answers it. An FBI agent in a sharp suit and fedora appears, special agent* NGUYEN. LENORE *freezes a bit.*

NGUYEN: Lenore Thomson?

LENORE: What?

NGUYEN: Is. . . ?

LENORE: This isn't a good time. Can you come back tomorrow?

NGUYEN: I'm afraid it's rather urgent.

Beat. She stares at him.

May I come inside?

LENORE: I'm baking a pie.

NGUYEN: Of course.

Beat. He's not going to leave.

LENORE: Fine. Follow me, please.

> *She disappears into the kitchen.* NGUYEN *takes a few steps to follow her, then stops. He looks in one of the packed boxes, containing children's toys. He examines a picture still hanging in the foyer with curiosity.* LENORE *rushes back.*

Please don't touch anything, just. . . follow me. The kitchen. My pie.

He follows her to the kitchen. Stops.

NGUYEN: Your name.

LENORE: What?

NGUYEN: Lenore. Thomson.

LENORE: *(smiles)* "Thomson" is from my husband, you understand. And "Lenore" is care of my very loving adoptive parents who just didn't know what to name a Chinese baby. . . but who had a great affinity for the works of Edgar Allan Poe.

NGUYEN: Of course. Just. . . surprising, is all.

LENORE: You can call me Mei-Ling or something, if it makes you feel better.

NGUYEN: No. No. . . I'm sorry. *(offering his hand)* Special Agent Nguyen, I'm with the FBI.

Beat. LENORE *ignores his proffered hand.*

LENORE: Is this about the parking tickets? Because I paid those.

NGUYEN: Parking tickets aren't. . . aren't really our purview.

LENORE: *(musing)* No, I didn't think so. *(a change of tactic)* How rude of me, can I offer you something to drink, Officer?

NGUYEN: Agent. No, thank you.

Beat. Then beginning his prepared speech.

Mrs. Thomson—

LENORE: Lenore, please. Everyone just calls me Lenore. Like the poem.

NGUYEN: Right.

LENORE: Do you know it?

NGUYEN: I think you may want to sit down.

LENORE: I'm okay standing, need to attend to the pie and—

NGUYEN gently ushers LENORE down to the chair.

NGUYEN: Please.

He removes his hat and holds it in front of him.

Mrs. Thomson—

LENORE: Lenore.

NGUYEN: —I regret to inform you that your son, Calder Thomson. . . was recently identified among the victims of the 2004 tsunami.

Beat. LENORE gets up.

LENORE: I forgot the cinnamon.

She goes to the pie to add cinnamon.

NGUYEN: I'm very sorry.

Beat.

I can call someone. If you need—

LENORE: It's been four years. Four years he's been missing. Why has it been. . .

NGUYEN: There are. . . thousands. . . still unidentified. Processing those—and because of his young age, you understand, the records aren't—I'm very sorry.

LENORE: Well, thank you for letting me know.

NGUYEN: I'm sorry.

LENORE: Please stop saying that.

NGUYEN: I'm—yes. Of course.

LENORE: I'm not someone inexperienced with loss, Officer. There were five of us who left here that winter: Myself, my son Calder, my husband and my parents. Only I came home. So I am very familiar with loss.

Beat.

But it's been four years. It's difficult to hold hope in your heart for four years. It wasn't built for that kind of long-term storage. It fades away, bit by bit, day by day. . . until you wake up one morning and it simply isn't there anymore. Just this. . . empty thing.

NGUYEN: Would you like me to call someone? We have a chaplain—

LENORE: I'm not religious. I find the less you believe in, the less that can disappoint you. Now, if we're quite finished—

She begins ushering him out.

NGUYEN: There's something. . .

LENORE stops.

LENORE: Something?

NGUYEN: Another reason I'm here.

LENORE: If it can wait until tomorrow, there's pie and. . . other things. Errands. Really, tomorrow would be so much more. . .

He stands his ground. LENORE deflates a bit.

Get on with it, then.

NGUYEN: Lenore, can you tell me what you were doing in Thailand that year?

LENORE: It was. . . a surprise. For my birthday. I was turning thirty and. . . devastated. . . about it. So my husband surprised me with a vacation. Our first family vacation. He booked us into a grand hotel, spent *way* too much. I. . .

90

She gets lost for a second.

I was so mad at him for spending so much money.

NGUYEN: And how long were you meant to stay?

She snaps out of it.

LENORE: One week.

NGUYEN: But you were there. . . an extraordinary amount of time, in the end. Two months, after the incident.

LENORE: An "incident"? I remember when it was still a "tragedy."

NGUYEN: Of course. . . If I could just ask you. . . Calder was. . . how old?

LENORE: *(suspicious)* Three.

> NGUYEN *takes a sheet of paper from his pocket and hands it to* LENORE. *She opens it.*

NGUYEN: This is a passenger manifest for your return flight to Salt Lake. The airline moved two tickets, one for you and one for Calder.

LENORE: They were purchased together, that makes sense.

NGUYEN: Of course it does, of course. . . what doesn't make sense. . . is that it says both you and Calder were on the flight home. His ticket and his passport were both scanned and registered.

Beat. Then another. LENORE *furrows her brow.*

You understand that set off a red flag when we identified his body. It. . . well, it raised some questions.

LENORE: Of course. Now, I'm just trying to. . . what was his name?

NGUYEN: Whose name?

LENORE: The young boy who flew with me. Leung? Chung?. . . Dammit.

NGUYEN: Mrs. Thomson—

LENORE: Lenore. Please. Like the poem. *"The sweet Lenore hath 'gone before,' with Hope, that flew beside."* Now what was his name?

NGUYEN: I'm afraid I don't—

LENORE: There was so much going on. Families were. . . stranded. The American Consular couldn't be reached. People had lost passports and all sorts of things. This young boy—about Calder's age—and his mother. . . "Chun"?

"Kung". . . ? They were trying to get back home—California if I remember correctly—but the boy didn't have his passport. I had Calder's, and his plane ticket. . . I was doing a good deed.

NGUYEN: So. . .

LENORE: So?

NGUYEN: You allowed this woman—

LENORE: "Wong," maybe?

NGUYEN: —to use your son's documents to get back in the country?

LENORE: Only the boy, the woman had her own papers.

NGUYEN *flusters.*

NGUYEN: Mrs. Thomson—

LENORE: Lenore.

NGUYEN: —what you did was. . . *severely* illegal. . . it's—

LENORE: I was helping, Officer. This poor woman and her son, they were in a situation. A real *situation*, you understand. My mother always used to say, "We have to be kind, in times like those. We must not be cruel."

NGUYEN: There is a difference between cruelty and prudence.

LENORE: And mercy? What of mercy, then?

NGUYEN: I understand you were in a state of shock and—yes, the psychological—but this is not a time for semantics. You committed a felony offence.

Beat.

LENORE: You "understand"? You're telling me that you. . . "understand."

Short beat.

NGUYEN: Of course not. I'm sorry.

LENORE: I lost *everyone*. Everyone I had in this world. Do you know what that is? To have that taken from you? Can you tell me you understand what that is?

Beat.

NGUYEN: I can't. . . I should leave.

LENORE pounces on this, pulls his arm towards the door.

LENORE: The door is straight through here, and if you want to come back—tomorrow, or next week, even—it's just not a good time right now, like I said. This has all been very exhausting, I'm quite tired, so if you'll just. . .

He isn't leaving. Beat.

This isn't Beckett, Officer, if you *say* you're leaving you—

NGUYEN: I want to sympathize. . . I *do* sympathize. . . and I'm sorry I have to—

LENORE: You're like a dog uncovering a bone; you keep scratching at me.

NGUYEN: What were you doing for two months in Thailand?

LENORE: Trying to find my son!

NGUYEN: Were you?

LENORE: Of course—

NGUYEN: Or were you taking other measures?

Beat.

LENORE: I don't—

NGUYEN: You flew to Bangkok for three weeks. Why?

LENORE: I—

NGUYEN: If you were looking, even if you were just *grieving,* why would you fly to Bangkok for so long?

LENORE: I—I got sick—very sick—food poisoning, the hospital was overloaded so I flew to Bangkok.

NGUYEN: For food poisoning?

LENORE: Yes.

NGUYEN: For three weeks?

LENORE: Yes!

> *Beat.*

What?

> *Beat.*

NGUYEN: So many *luk-kreung*—half-children, like Calder—looking for their parents. You must have seen his face. . . everywhere. So many of them in the aftermath. . . there'd be no way to tell when they were ushered into homes or. . . into trucks. . . carted away.

Taken away. . . to be sold.

LENORE: If you are implying. . . adoption—

NGUYEN: Abduction.

LENORE: I resent the idea that. . . I can't even conceive of *what* idea—

NGUYEN: You stay in Thailand for two months. You fly back with a passenger who is now confirmed as—I'm sorry—as *dead*, Lenore. This house, those pictures. . . pictures of a child of at least six, not three. Toys, *new* toys, in those boxes by the door. I need you to tell me what happened.

LENORE: I *have* told you!

Beat. NGUYEN *looks at her.*

You are not the man you first appeared to be. You have. . . duplicity, Officer—

NGUYEN: Agent.

LENORE: Duplicity!

Beat.

You are a cavity inside a new veneer. But I can see you now. Rotting and. . . decaying everything with your—your accusations. You cannot *accuse* people of things, not when they've just—not when they've lost what I've lost. Chameleon. Chimera. Shame on you for changing skins on me.

Beat.

NGUYEN: Your pie is burning.

> LENORE *takes a deep breath in. She rescues the pie from the oven, holds it a minute, then pitches it—viciously and wordlessly—at the wall beside* NGUYEN's *head. It slides down to the floor.* NGUYEN *is unfazed.* LENORE *takes another breath. She sits opposite him and looks him dead in the eye.*

LENORE: Excuse the mess. I'm packing everything up. I'm leaving, you see. I won a contest. A contest to go and live somewhere far away from here. We're leaving tonight. Calder and I. . . we're leaving tonight. And we'll be so far away you'll never hear from us again. We'll just leave. You don't even have to know. You can just come to the door tomorrow and I won't be here. It happens. Things like that. They happen.

NGUYEN: Calder? You gave him. . . his name, you call him by his name?

LENORE: I just. . . wanted him back. I didn't want to be alone.

NGUYEN: It isn't *him*, this *boy* isn't—

LENORE: Just come back tomorrow! It's one day, not even that, it's. . . it's twelve hours.

Beat.

We were both orphaned that day, but we found each other. I provide for him; I am not negligent or abusive; I am a woman of means and I *love* him. He has the opportunity to be anything if he's with me. What would his life have been there? A fishing village? He deserves so much more. What I had. He deserves what I had.

NGUYEN: He deserves a life of his own, not a. . . to be a replacement. He's a person, not a thing.

Beat.

LENORE: Do you know that the sheer force of the earth that day moved the ground here in Utah? Eleven thousand miles away, did you know that?

NGUYEN *shakes his head no.*

Right here, in this neighbourhood, the ground shifted upwards by one millimetre. It's true, it was in the paper. And you don't even notice. Everything looks the same, not even a jar off the shelf. . . but an entire neighbourhood has been changed. And when you say it that way, it sounds so much more dramatic. . . dire, even. But it was just one millimetre. That's all. Who would notice that? If no one said anything, if it wasn't in the paper. . . who would notice something so small?

Beat.

Do you have children, Agent?

NGUYEN: I. . . yah.

LENORE: And do they mean everything to you?

NGUYEN: Mrs. Thomson—

LENORE: What would you have done?

Beat. He is not going to answer. LENORE *slumps.*

NGUYEN: I'm sorry, Mrs. Thomson.

LENORE: *(far away now)* Lenore. . . like the poem.

He gently stands LENORE *up, cradling her hands in his.*
A moment of softness, uncertainty.

NGUYEN: *For her, the fair and* debonair, *that now so lowly lies,*
The life upon her yellow hair but not within her eyes—

LENORE: *The life still there, upon her hair—the death upon*
her eyes.

Beat. A slight, wry half-smile

You do know it. . .

NGUYEN's *hand reaches for his handcuffs. A pause. A*
break. A moment of something inside. He replaces his
hands on LENORE's. *He grips her hard. A struggle.*

NGUYEN: Yah. Yah, I know it.

They stare at one another. A wordless stalemate. They are each immovable. They are each in check.

THE VERMIN STORY

Ko Phi Phi Island, Thailand. The present. Sound of waves. Gentle. DIEGO *Garcia is sitting on the beach. He looks out into the water, deep in thought. Suddenly, a man is beside him.*

VERMIN: They say a movie ruined this beach. You know that movie? With the good-looking kid from *Titanic* and that Scottish guy? Terrible movie. Anyway, after it came out, tourists came by the hundreds. . . thousands, now, probably. It used to be pristine.

Beat. No response from DIEGO.

Ah, but I was here back before the movie, before the book, even. Maybe before that, when the author was still a young man and full of hope. . . maybe then it was a paradise.

Beat.

Still, it beats Yangon.

DIEGO: I like Yangon.

VERMIN: *(shrugs)* Crowded.

Beat.

You know, there's a storm coming. You can see it if you look hard, a few miles out.

Beat.

My mother used to say the rain and the lightning were caused by the two brothers still fighting over the throne of Heaven.

DIEGO: Look, pal, I don't have any money on me.

VERMIN: Oh, I wasn't going to ask.

He looks down at his dirty, tattered clothes.

I suppose I understand your mistake, though. It's laundry day.

DIEGO: Right. Well. . . look, I kinda wanted to be alone here.

VERMIN: Pretend I'm not here. I can be very quiet. I learned during military raids back home.

DIEGO: It's a big beach, pal.

VERMIN: Isn't it, though? Beautiful. Expansive. . . oh, that's a word, isn't it? Yes. . .

DIEGO: I don't mean to be rude, but—

VERMIN: No, it is I who am rude.

He extends his hand.

My name is Mr. Vermin.

DIEGO *begrudgingly shakes his hand.*

DIEGO: Garcia. Diego Garcia.

VERMIN: I like that. Like, "Bond, James Bond."

DIEGO: I guess.

Beat.

Your English.

VERMIN *looks at him.*

It's good.

VERMIN: *(shrugs)* You need me to speak English. So I speak English. Amazing, I know.

Beat. VERMIN *nods to the rosary* DIEGO *is holding.*

You've been praying.

DIEGO: Hah. No. . . no, I just found this. Under the sand, here.

VERMIN: May I?

DIEGO *tosses him the rosary.*

DIEGO: S'all yours.

VERMIN *examines it.*

VERMIN: My thanks. I believe it's exactly what I've been looking for.

He pockets the rosary.

DIEGO: Now, if you don't mind. . .

VERMIN: Why are you out here?

DIEGO: I'm sightseeing, just like everyone else.

VERMIN: You know what happened here?

VERMIN *waves out to the Indian Ocean.*

Out there?

Beat.

DIEGO: People died.

VERMIN: Yes, they did.

VERMIN shakes his head.

Terrible. People here. . . they are trying to move on, but some of them. . . some just can't. You know how that is?

DIEGO: Yah. Yah, I know how that is.

VERMIN: So these people. . . they get distressed. Easily, most. They are. . . searching. . . for something. A reason. An answer. Something to lay blame on. So how do you think people react to a man who comes to their beach, who comes to *every* beach, sits on the sand. . . for days, sometimes. And when people ask why he's there, he tells them—

DIEGO: They died because of me.

Beat.

VERMIN: What sort of man says something like that? To people like that? Who've been through what they have.

DIEGO: A guilty man.

VERMIN: No. No, guilt is a funnier thing. It makes one hide in corners like a rat. Furtive. Ever seen a rat sit on a beach for days? No. This is a desperate man. To be sure.

DIEGO: Sure.

VERMIN: But people are funny. They hear a man say he's guilty, and they think *he's guilty*. Isn't that funny?

DIEGO: Not really.

VERMIN: No, I suppose not. Because the next thing that happens is that those people begin asking for retribution. They demand it. They *need* it. And when it comes to what people *need*, Mr. Garcia. . . well, that's where I come in.

> VERMIN *removes a Glock pistol from the waistband of his pants, weighs it in his hand.*

Guilty or not, something has to be done about you.

> *Beat.*

But hold on a second, I tell them, *I haven't even met this man.* So here I am. You seem pleasant enough. Not unsound, mentally, from all appearances. Good-looking. . . if you like that sort of thing. So?

> *He raises the pistol.*

Anything I should know?

Beat.

DIEGO: I work. . . used to work, at the PTWC in Hawaii. There was a quake, on the twenty-third, on the border of the Indian Ocean. I sent out a warning to the coastal areas that there was danger of tsunami activity. That turned out to be false. And that wasn't a small quake, that was a 7.8. But nothing happened. I was working again, on the twenty-sixth, when the Sumatra quake hit. At first, it measured an 8.0. And after. . .

He trails off.

VERMIN: Yes. . . ?

DIEGO: I released a bulletin that said: "No destructive tsunami threat exists."

I didn't know.

It wasn't an 8.0. It turned out to be a 9.2. The third largest earthquake in *history*. And I'm the guy who told everyone to go back to sleep, it was probably nothing.

I guessed.

Over a quarter of a million people died that day because I *guessed* at something I didn't know.

He turns to face VERMIN.

I stopped going to work. I left Hawaii. I've been to every place that goddamn water touched. I've sat on every beach from here to Somalia. And do you think I've cried?

VERMIN: Any man would.

DIEGO: Not me. Not one tear. Nothing to give.

> DIEGO *walks closer to* VERMIN, *almost right up to the pistol.*

So just. . . just do it. You want someone to answer for this? It's me. Me alone.

Beat. VERMIN *lowers the pistol a bit.*

VERMIN: Stop me if you've heard this one: A man is stranded in a flood. He's a faithful man, so he prays to God to rescue him. The water keeps rising, the man has to climb on the roof of his house, and then a rescue boat shows up and they invite the man on board. He says, "No, God will rescue me." The boat goes off to rescue his neighbour. A little while later, water still rising, up to his neck now—a hovercraft comes by. They tell him to get on board, he says, "No, God will rescue me." They leave as well. Finally, the man is treading water and a helicopter lowers a rope down. They yell at him to take it, he says, "No, God will rescue me." The man drowns. When he gets to Heaven, he asks

God, "Why didn't you rescue me?" God says, "I sent you a boat, a hovercraft and a helicopter. . . what do you want from me?"

DIEGO laughs.

DIEGO: So, what. . . you're telling me God sent you?

VERMIN shakes his head.

VERMIN: Do you see a boat. . . or a helicopter?

VERMIN smiles.

No. . . I'm telling you there is no God. We have to save ourselves. We're men. We're only men.

DIEGO: Uplifting.

VERMIN: Sorry.

Beat. VERMIN looks out at the horizon, at the approaching storm.

I'm convinced now. Of what you need, now. Of the crime. Of the punishment. But you've got some time, yet. You've got. . . until the storm comes. . . okay?

DIEGO nods. As VERMIN talks, the light slowly fades; day turning to night, maybe. Maybe an eclipse. Maybe the shadow of some giant.

VERMIN: I was fishing when it happened. Off the coast of Burma, where I had grown up, lived all my life. Do you know that if you are far enough out on the ocean, away from land, the waves will pass right under you and you won't even notice? You rise and fall with them, but it is. . . gentle, almost.

I was not far enough out to experience this. But I am told this is the way. I was closer. I still didn't notice the waves until I started moving on them. Until suddenly I was backwards, stern to bow and rushing towards land. I don't know how I stayed afloat, I don't know. . . why. . . I didn't capsize like the others. Maybe. . . maybe this was something I was meant to see. Maybe this was punishment for everything I had done wrong.

Beat.

Thirty-eight. I was thirty-eight.

I rode in on the wave like one of the four horsemen. A harbinger of death, a rider on the storm. I saw nothing at first, nothing but water and a sliver of horizon. Then, like on the shoulders of this impossible giant, from a great height. . . I saw land. A beach. Then trees. Buildings. Then. . . then I saw people. I saw their faces. And I thought. . .

Beat.

People have such friendly faces.

Then I passed out.

I woke up on one of the main roads in Thailand. Kilometres inland. My boat was nowhere to be seen. I woke up beside another man, an enormous gash across his face. A face I didn't know, but looked familiar, somehow. I found his identity card in his back pocket and started calling his name at him. Pumping on his chest, crying, yelling his name. . . but he would not answer. Later I would examine the card and realize the man and myself were born on the same day of the same year. He was thirty-eight years old.

I passed out again.

This time I awake in a Thai hospital. Faces all around. New faces. The dead and the living moving in and out of rooms so quickly. Faces everywhere. Strange faces. And I begin to notice something I've never paid attention to before. I start to really *look* at people.

Pretend you are in a hospital. Or a busy street. Or in a theatre. Pretend you are in a theatre and you're sitting next to people you haven't met. Now, maybe someone asks the time, and you tell him it's almost 8:00, the show should be starting soon. He nods and you go back to your lives. And you don't even notice that this man bears a striking resemblance to your father. Even to you. You will never know that the man was born in the same hospital you were. You won't know if he has children at home, waiting for him. . . or if he lives alone, or what he watches on television before he goes to sleep. You won't know this man contracted a rare blood disease on vacation in Maldives. You will never know that the hospital he goes to will experience a shortage of his blood type for transfusion. And so you won't know when this man dies. And then it will truly be of no consequence that the blood he needed courses in your veins. Because he only ever asked you the time. And you only ever told him it was 8:00. The show should be starting soon.

This is what I think about in the hospital. It is, I think, the saddest day of my life.

Beat.

But consider, for a moment, that we live in a world of magic and inexplicable serendipity, and that anything is possible. And in that world of hope and possibility, I turn to the woman in the bed to my right. I think of all the faces I have seen, those passing me on the street, brushing right up against my shoulder, whose names I never learned. I say, "What is your name." She tells me.

She wants to know where her daughter is. If she's safe. She shows me a picture of a young girl. Her face is red from the sun and she's smiling the smile of an eighteen-year-old who has never been touched by tragedy.

"I'm sorry," I say, "I remember your daughter. I saw her face." I had, on the shoulders of that giant. I saw that eighteen-year-old smile turn into something that is burned into my eyes. Right into my eyes. The woman cries. And she cries. And then she says, "Thank you."

Consider that I am Burmese receiving Thai care, and every time a police officer comes through the hospital I turn my face. But they are coming now, checking papers, Thai on one side, Burmese on the other. Many Burmese, I hadn't even realized. They are being put in a corner, my brothers, to be taken first to jail, then back across the border. Back to the dirt and the rot. A uniform is in front of me now, asking for papers. My heart stops. I look at my brothers. Now consider that I still have, clutched in my hand for days, the dead man's identity card. The man who I would only realize just now looks remarkably like myself. I hand it to the officer. He is suspicious. He asks the woman, "Do you know this man?" The woman is crying. He asks her again. "Do you know this man?"

Finally she nods.

And like that. . . I am free.

Consider in the days that follow I speak to every person in that hospital. I find that if I look at them, really *look* at them. . . I know what it is they need. And I find it. I always find it. It is my gift. In this world touched by curse, the man who rode on the harbinger's shoulder is now. . . is now their guide. Their way back home.

Consider this could all be legend. That a man with such a gift could never actually exist, not in this world. Consider it could be a morality tale, inspiring us to think of what we could achieve if we just helped our brothers and sisters. If we just looked at one another. If we just cared what one another truly needs. Consider this could only be a fraction of reality, and it is probably best left never investigated. . . because what truth we find in hope often pales to the hope we might have gained to begin with.

But consider also that, like anything, this is a story that might be true.

> *Beat. The storm has arrived. It is torrential, flood-like, even Biblical.*

Because we are all connected.

> *He takes up the gun, presses it against* DIEGO's *head.*

And we are, none of us, alone.

> *Suddenly,* DIEGO *collapses in* VERMIN's *arms. He begins to cry, softly at first, then weeping.* VERMIN *lets the gun fall as he cradles the other man's head. He cries in the tide. Centuries of tears pour down his face, washing over them both, taking them out to sea. Carrying them away. Out and away.*

> *Blackout.*

> *End of play.*

ACKNOWLEDGEMENTS

This work has been developed and supported by: Native Earth Performing Arts, fu-GEN Theatre Company, the Toronto Arts Council, the Ontario Arts Council and the Canada Council for the Arts. In 2009, the play found its home at Tarragon Theatre under the generous watch of Richard Rose and Andrea Romaldi, and was completed while in residence there.

Many of those who spoke to me and told me their stories did so under the condition of anonymity, which I will uphold. For those who didn't: Kwan Sr. and Jr., Lovisa, Jasmine J., Yogesh, Yine, Manny, Risa, Han, all three Muhammads, and the cab driver in Phuket whose name I didn't catch but sounded like "Rocco". . . my sincere gratitude for being generous and open and trusting me with your stories.

Special thanks to my brilliant partner-in-art Nina, to Richard and Andrea, Stanton, Anita, Yvette, Helen and Suzanne, all the workshop actors over the years, and the final cast and creative team on the Tarragon production for their invaluable input and feedback during the development of this script. I'm in your debt.

And to Jasmine, Sue, Pepper and Gypsy. . . thanks for holding me together. I rely on you more than any grown man should.

David Yee is an actor and playwright and the artistic director of fu-GEN Asian Canadian Theatre Company. His other plays include *lady in the red dress*, which was nominated for the 2010 Governor General's Literary Award for Drama, and *paper SERIES*. He lives in Toronto.

First edition: October 2014
Printed and bound in Canada by Imprimerie Gauvin, Gatineau

Cover design by Leon Aureus

PLAYWRIGHTS
CANADA PRESS

202-269 Richmond Street West
Toronto, ON
M5V 1X1

416.703.0013
info@playwrightscanada.com
playwrightscanada.com

RECYCLED
Paper made from
recycled material
FSC
www.fsc.org   FSC® C100212